"Grizabella, meet your babies."

He must have heard me wrong.

What he did next was (and this is almost too awful for words so if you're easily grossed out, put this book down and walk away now) he went over to one of his babies.

Before anyone could stop him, Grizabella ate it.

In one glump.

"Grizabella!" I yelled as I grabbed him and pulled him away,

"I said 'meet your babies' not 'eat your babies'!"

I tried not to take that as a sign that he was a terrible parent.

Leena
and the Gerbils

The Leena series by Elaine Miskinis

Leena and the Gerbils

Leena and the Thinking Tree (coming soon!)

To Abby,

Leena
and the Gerbils

by Elaine Miskinis
illustrated by Lorrie Moore

Happy Reading! ☺

Ea

ISBN-13: 978-1502760081

Hayden,

Your insistence on nightly "real life" stories

brought life to this book.

Without you there would be no story.

(Sorry about the worms.)

Kaya,

Your spirited energy and your unique ideas

are a constant source of inspiration.

This book is for you both.

Contents

The Week Before

Mom always tells me that I jump into the middle of stories and I talk too fast and I don't always make sense.

So, I'm going to start from the beginning so you'll understand why gerbils are such a big deal for a girl whose only pets up until now have been two dead worms named Slinky and Slimy.

My name is Leena Fogg and I'm in first
grade, almost second, at Cherrydale
Elementary School. My school doesn't
have cherry trees. Or cherry pies.
Or anything with cherries at all.

This feels like false advertising to me.

My mom says that names don't always
mean anything and I guess that's true.
My last name is Fogg and I don't even

know how a person can be fog.
Or drizzle, or any weather actually.
Mom sometimes says my room looks like
a tornado hit it, so maybe that counts.

But still, some names should just fit.
Like Cherrydale. They could at least
make an effort to give us cherries now
and then.

These are the kinds of things that make
school frustrating.

I liked first grade all right. I learned how
to play a recorder. Mostly I just got it
to make the kinds of sounds a dying
snake probably makes, but that was fun
and Mom and Dad stood up and clapped
for me at the Winter Concert.

It doesn't take much to make them
proud.

Now that summer is almost here some kids are talking about going camping or taking trips or just running around like crazy until fall.

But, from the minute Mrs. Moore told us that she was going to need someone to take the class gerbils home for the summer, I knew how I wanted to spend my summer.

I wouldn't say I'm a natural with pets exactly, but I kind of blame my parents for that. We don't have a cat named Butterscotch like my best friend Molly, or even a turtle.

We have nothing. Not even a stupid fish that can't even do tricks. The only experience I've ever had with pets were Slinky and Slimy. And that's a sad story.

You see, we were doing a project in Sunday school about the circle of life and how we're all connected to nature, even to the dirt.

We got to scoop up dirt and mush it around, which was pretty fun, and way better than sitting in a chair trying to be peaceful, which I'm not very good at.

In the end we all got worms to take home, I guess so we'd all remember that we're part of dirt.

I named my worms Slinky and Slimy. It was hard to tell which one was which because they moved around so much.

I asked Mom if I could use a Sharpie and write their names on them to make it easier, but she said no. I should have known then that she didn't really care about them the way I did.

I took them home in their glass jar with holes punched in the lid and I put them on my dresser. They were fine for a while. But, then one afternoon Mom was putting away clothes in my room when the phone rang.

She says that what happened next was an accident. But I'm not so sure. All I know is that my folded sweaters ended up on top of the jar.

For a week.

It was Saturday when Mom told me I had to pick up my room and put my clothes away.

That's when I saw.

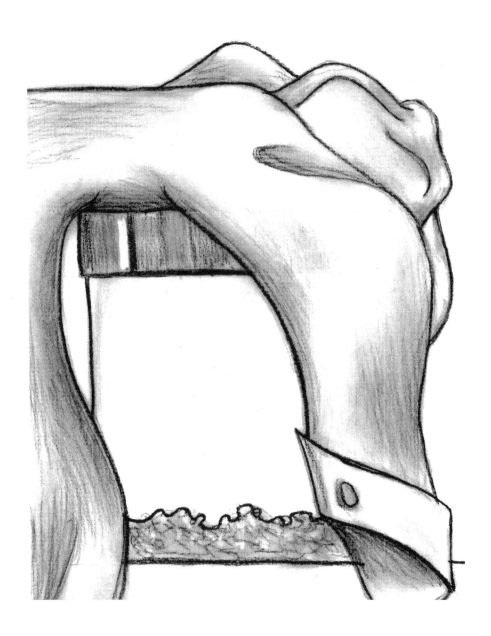

The air holes in the jar had been covered for days. Mom tried to say that if I had put my clothes away earlier they may have survived.

But, I think it was all part of her plan to live in a pet-free house. And, maybe to make me feel a little bad about the way my room looks. I'm not sure about that second part.

But, I do know that Mom never really bonded with Slinky and Slimy the way I hoped she would.

I don't like to think about what happened to Slinky and Slimy. It was terrible. I buried them in the backyard by the shed and I played my recorder for them.

I think **Slinky** and **Slimy** would have
appreciated dead snake sounds. It's the
music of their people.

For a long time after **Slinky** and **Slimy** I thought that we'd never have another pet.

Only now I had a mission.

These gerbils needed a proper home for the summer, and I was the one for the job.

Besides, Mom couldn't kill gerbils with laundry. Right?

Week One

"Mom. I want a horse."

Mom looked up from her magazine and turned her head to the side a little bit.

"A horse? Where is this coming from?"

"Well, we have room in the back yard and Dad never did anything with the shed out there. It just makes sense really."

"No, it doesn't," she said. Then she went back to reading.

This was all part of my plan. When it comes to Mom, it's always best to start big and then take it down a notch.
I've seen Dad do it a million times.

Last winter he wanted to get a new snow blower because the old one made him say words that aren't okay for kids to hear.

He wanted a snow blower, so he told Mom he needed a new truck with a plow. She made that deep sigh she sometimes makes and said something about payments and how he always thinks he needs new toys.

This is funny because a truck is not a toy. Not even a little bit. You can't sit behind the steering wheel and pretend you're driving off a cliff or you get in a lot of trouble.

I know this.

But, Dad said he needed a truck so that Mom would think a snow blower wasn't a big deal. And sure enough, a week later he came home with a brand new snow blower.

Now most of the time I can have my
friends over to build snowmen while he
takes care of the driveway. And we
don't get so many calls from other
parents about Dad's language anymore.

I knew that the first step in getting a
gerbil would be asking for a horse.
Not that I wouldn't love to have a
horse, but for now it was all about

asking for something big so a gerbil wouldn't seem like such a bad deal.

I call it compromising. My mom uses a different word, "manipulation," and she says I learned it from my dad.

I poured my cereal and I put on my best "you never let me get anything" face.

Mom wasn't looking at me at all except to make sure I didn't pour milk all over the table, but I kept my sad face on just the same.

I knew it was a long shot, since Mom doesn't really care about faces. I know this because whenever I get in trouble I try to do my best "cute kid" face and the only time it ever works is when she doesn't feel like being mad anyway.

Dad was already at work but I knew he wouldn't be a lot of help anyway. He always says, "It's your call, Barb" and then my mom does what she was going to do anyway.

"If I can't get a horse, how about a cat?" I asked. "Everyone has a cat."

Mom looked up from her paper again. "You need to finish your cereal and find some shoes," she said. She got up to put her coffee mug in the sink. "And not everyone has a cat," she said. "Look at us. We don't."

Sometimes that woman is just plain unkind.

When I got to school the first thing I did was run to the gerbil cage so I could see those two bits of fluffy goodness.

One of them was running on the gerbil wheel making the best "squeak, squeak" sound in the world. The other was sucking on a long metal gerbil straw that led to a water bottle at the top of the cage.

Gerbil cages are like their own magical worlds of greatness. I mean, who wouldn't want to fluff around in wood chips and run on a squeaky wheel all day?

Suddenly, from behind me, I heard a voice. "I can't wait to have those gerbils for the summer."

I turned around.

Mark Pitts was standing right behind me.

Mark Pitts.

There are some things you need to know about Mark Pitts. He kicks kids under the seat on the bus. And last month he took my fluffy key chain off of my backpack to "look at it" and then he broke the link so now it's not even a key chain anymore. You can't trust the lives of two gerbils to a boy like that.

20

"They're not yours, Mark Pitts," I told him. "Mrs. Moore hasn't said who is getting them."

"Well, it's not going to be you," Mark Pitts shot back. "Didn't you kill your pet worms?"

Mom's right when she says I overshare.

I wondered if Mrs. Moore remembered that story. Probably she did. I had written about it in my Writer's Journal just a week before. I even drew a picture of the worm graveyard.

What if Mrs. Moore thought that I was a pet killer? That would be even worse than being Mark Pitts who breaks things. I was going to need to work hard to get Mrs. Moore to see that I was the best choice for gerbil hosting.

Mark Pitts was tapping on the cage. "Here gerbil, gerbil, gerbil. Come on Fluffy," he said.

I walked away and sat down at my desk.
I would need to come up with a plan.
The best plan ever.

A plan that would make a gerbil proud.

Week Two

I sat down at my desk and I opened my Writer's Notebook.

I thought about ripping out the pages about Slinky and Slimy, but Mrs. Moore had already read them. I could tell because there was a sticker on top that said, "Way to Go!"

I wasn't sure if the sticker was congratulating me for killing the worms, or if she just didn't have stickers that said, "I'm sorry for your loss".
Or, maybe she meant it like, "Way to go, you worm killer you," the way Dad sometimes says "Good job" in his grumpy voice when his team misses a pass.

I just couldn't tell.

I opened to a new page and I started to write.

> Today is June 16th. I am the best person for the gerbils because I will not kill them. I do not ever kill animals at all and the worms were not my fault. Mark Pitts breaks things and he taps on glass. He also kicks on the bus. I need to have these gerbils to bring joy to my life. And also because the wheel makes a squeaky sound.

I put my pencil down.

It was brilliant.

I had stated my case and now all I had to do was wait for Mrs. Moore to read it, give me a big, strong hug, and then pack up those gerbils and send them my way.

"Mrs. Moore! Mrs. Moore!" I waved my arms in the air until she came over to my desk.

"What is it Leena?" she asked.

"I wrote something in my Writer's Journal," I told her.

"That's fantastic. We'll be doing more writing after lunch. Maybe you can share it with the group then."

I knew that by lunchtime Mark Pitts would probably have packed up those gerbils and headed for the hills.

"You need to read it now," I insisted. "It's really important."

Mrs. Moore slid my journal over in front of her. I watched her eyes as she read it, but they didn't even tear up at all. That woman is made of stone.

"I see," she said finally. She pushed the journal back to my side of the desk. "You make a strong case for those gerbils," she told me, "but the final decision is up to your parents. If your family decides that you want to take the gerbils for the summer, have them get in touch."

"But what about Mark Pitts?" I asked. We both looked over at him.

He had moved on from the gerbils and was now spinning the globe in the corner of the room as fast as he could.

"It's first come, first serve," Mrs. Moore said. "Whoever asks first will get to take the gerbils home."

"I see," I said.

I put on my best, "I'm turning green here" face before clutching my stomach.

"I think I'm coming down with something," I said. "I might need to go home. Now."

The school nurse took my temperature and she had me lay down on a cot with a paper cover. It sounded like a doctor's office when I rolled around.

It's hard to pretend to be sick when you can roll and make paper crunch sounds with your body.

"Well, you don't have a temperature," the nurse said.

"Sometimes people get bitten by snakes and they don't get temperatures. They just turn black and get puffy and then if they don't get help they can die," I informed her. "I saw it on Discovery Channel."

"Were you bitten by a snake, dear?" the nurse asked.

I shook my head 'no'.

"Why don't you have a drink of water and head back to class," she said.

It was going to be a very long day.

Week Three

When I got home that afternoon I still didn't have a plan. I needed to think fast if I was going to get this locked down before Mark Pitts got his parents to agree to being the gerbils' host family.

I could just picture Mark Pitts kicking his parents under the table at dinner and telling them that he'd hold his breath until he turned blue if they didn't let him take the gerbils.

That's exactly the kind of kid he was.

I would never stoop so low. Not unless I thought it would work. And it wouldn't. My mom likes those kinds of challenges.

One time I told her I'd stand on one foot all day if she didn't let me wear my pink sparkle shoes to the dump.

She took the shoes from me and said, "Go for it". I made it about twenty minutes on one foot, which is a feat I tell you.

Get it. A feat?

Anyway, holding my breath seemed like a bad way to play it with my mom. So did writing a letter. She's a stickler for proper grammar and punctuation, even more than Mrs. Moore is.

She doesn't believe in what she calls "that Kindergarten spelling nonsense," and I knew she'd make me fix everything in the letter.

The message would be lost on her.

So, in the end there was only one thing to do. Wait till Dad came home and then put it all out there during the one time in the day when they both give me their full attention.

It would have to happen during "Sad, Happy, Silly" dinner sharing time.

I was the perfect kid before dinner. I helped to set the table, and I didn't even complain about the fact that my favorite spoon with the dots was in the dishwasher.

Again.

And I didn't complain about the fact that we were out of the right dip for my crunchy carrots.

For the second day in a row.

Seriously, those people need to do a load of dishes and head to the store sometime. But, I didn't say that.

I even told Dad I liked his tie. That part was totally true too. It was the tie I got him for Christmas last year, the one with a big yellow lightning bolt on it.

He said it "adds flair" to his suit, but really I think he just hasn't done laundry in a while.

"This roast is delicious!" I said before I
even took a bite. I was afraid if I waited
until I tried it I wouldn't be able to
sound so sincere.

"Are you feeling okay?" Mom asked.

"Yup. Good as new," I said, not sure if
Mom had gotten a call from the nurse or
if she was just wondering why I was

being so agreeable. She gets suspicious when I'm too nice.

That woman does not always see the best in me.

"Who has a sad, happy or silly to share tonight?" Dad asked.

"I have a sad to share," said Mom. "One of my coworkers just found out that she has to move to Pittsburg for her husband's work".

My eyes got big at that news.

"The Pitts own a burg?" I asked.

There was no way I could compete with a family that owned a whole burg. I didn't even know what a burg was but it sounded big and important. That Mark Pitts had too many things going for him.

"What?" Mom asked. "Who are the Pitts?"

"The people who own the burg," I said with a sigh. "They own a burg and now they're going to get the gerbils, and Mark Pitts kicks on the bus, and it's just not fair." I started to cry.

Mom and Dad looked at each other.

"I'm sorry Honey, but you're going to need to back up a step here," Dad said. "Why don't you start from the beginning and help us understand what you're talking about."

"Mark Pitts is in my class and he kicks on the bus, and he broke my key chain and now he's going to get the class gerbils because his family owns a burg and they can get anything they want."

Mom sighed. "I think I get it now."

Dad still looked confused. It always takes him a bit longer.

Mom put down her fork. "First of all, Pittsburg is a city, and I highly doubt that Mark Pitts' family has any connection to it at all. They certainly don't own it. As for gerbils, I don't understand why you're so upset. You've never even mentioned gerbils."

I thought back to our conversations, to my master plan. I had asked for a horse, and then a cat, but I hadn't quite gotten to the gerbil part yet.

"I want to take home the class gerbils for the summer," I said, "but I know you won't let me."

"What makes you think that?" asked
Mom.

"Well, you killed Slinky and Slimy and
then you didn't even go to their funeral,
and then you said I couldn't have a
horse, or even a cat," I said, still
fighting back tears.

Mom and Dad looked at each other.

"Do you have a question to ask us?"
asked Mom.

I looked up and I didn't even have to put
on my sad begging face because it was
already kind of there.

"Can I take the class gerbils home for
the summer?" I asked.

"I don't see any problem with that," said
Mom. She looked at Dad.

"It's your call, Barb," he said.

I couldn't believe it. Sometimes parents are full of surprises.

I reached across the table to hug them both and it would have been a perfect moment if I hadn't spilled my milk all over the table.

Week Four

Carrying the gerbil cage out to the car on the last day of school I felt like a superstar.

Mark Pitts stood beside the sidewalk with his arms crossed. I almost went over and patted him on the shoulder, but I knew if he had gotten the gerbils and he came over to pat my shoulder I'd want to push him, so I decided that probably wasn't a good idea.

Plus, he kicked my feet on the bus and scuffed my socks so I wasn't really feeling all that kind myself.

Mom had to come pick me up from school to bring home the gerbils and all the stuff that went with them.

I really wanted to take them on the bus so they could look out the window and also so that everyone could say, "Leena, what do you have there?" and I could show off my new pets.

But, Mom said there was too much to carry and for once she was actually kind of right. There was food, a bag of sawdust to put on the floor of the cage for them to sleep in and poop on (hopefully not in the same place though).

They even came with a cool drip drink thing that hangs from the side of the cage so they can suck water down whenever they need it.

This was a big relief.

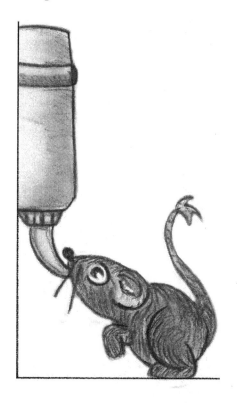

I sort of wish I knew about those when I had Slinky and Slimy.

Maybe it would have made a difference.

• • •

We took the gerbils to the car and placed them gently in the back seat.

"They need one of those balls they can run around in. And new names."

Mom looked at me. "This isn't going to be one of those things where we suddenly spend a ton of money on a pair of little furballs," she said.

This was why they needed new names, I decided.

Mom would be much more open to getting things for them if they had cuter names. Right now they were called

Furball and Snuffy. Not terrible, but not the kind of names that would make you run out and buy them a new running ball.

"Grizabella," I said.

"Grizabella?" Mom asked.

"Here's GRIZABELLA!" I said in my best carnival voice. "She's the cutest gerbil the world has ever seen. Just wait until you see the tricks I bet she can do!"

Mom rolled her eyes. "What about the other one?"

I looked at the gerbil formerly known as Snuffy for a long time.

"Floyd," I said finally.

"Floyd? Isn't it a girl?"

"Floyd is a perfectly good girl name," I said. "Besides, Dr. Floyd is the best dentist in the world."

"Dr. Floyd is a man," Mom said. "And, I might add, not a gerbil."

I gazed lovingly at little Floyd through the glass of her cage. "You just don't understand gerbils."

Week Five

"MOM!"

"MOM!"

I jumped out of bed and ran to my parents' room.

They had the air conditioner on, which explained why Mom hadn't gotten up right away when I yelled for her. They put their air conditioner on every single night even if it's not hot.

Mom says it's to keep the air fresh, but really I think she likes not being able to hear me when I call for her.

I think when you have a kid you should keep things quiet so you can be ready whenever they need you.

Mom doesn't agree.

. . .

I shook her shoulder gently and then I put my face right up against hers so that I could use my whisper voice and not wake up Daddy.

She opened her eyes and my eyeballs were right against hers. She shot straight up in bed.

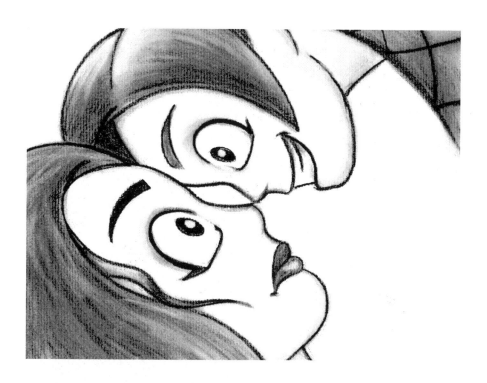

"Leena! You have to stop doing that!"

You'd really think she'd be used to it by now, but every time I come in her room, which is most nights, she zooms up like she's never seen my face close up before.

"Mommy, there's a monster in my room," I told her.

Calling her Mommy works best late at night when I need a drink of water, an extra tuck in or just some company.
It reminds her that I'm her little girl and that little girls are more important than sleep.

This is especially important when there's a real live monster in my bedroom and I need her to grab a baseball bat, follow me in there and take care of business.

"Do you have a bat?" I asked her.

"A what?" she said, rubbing her eyes.

"A bat. You know, a baseball bat, or maybe a softball bat, or I guess it could be a stick. To kill the monster."

She shook her head. "There's no monster in your room Leena. You need to go back to bed."

"You didn't even look. I'm telling you. There's a monster."

This wasn't like the night before when I forgot that I left my big stuffed dog, Dasher, at the foot of my bed and I woke up thinking it was a monster coming to get me.

Or even three nights ago when that pile of laundry in the corner looked like it was slinking across the room.

Or that other time when there really was a super scary sound that turned out to be the heat kicking in in May, which is crazy because May is practically summer and Mom had the air conditioner on.

But, Mom just said, "Darn polar vortex," and tucked me back in.

This time though it was real.

* * *

"Mom, it's going 'Eeek, Eeek, Eeek'. Nothing that's not a monster makes that sound."

Mom deep sighed and got up. She followed me to my room. Sure enough, there was that sound. "Eeek, Eeek, Eeek"

She walked over to my dresser and there, in the dark was Floyd, doing some laps on her gerbil wheel.

I don't know what kind of a health nut that gerbil is, but I will tell you that the "Eeek, Eeek, Eeek" of a squeaky wheel sounds an awful lot like the sound a monster would make in the middle of the night.

Mom reached into the cage and lifted the gerbil wheel out. She put it right next to the cage where Floyd could look at it but not play with it, which I thought was a bit unkind. And then she tucked me back into bed.

The next morning she moved the cage into the living room and my sleepovers with Floyd and Grizabella came to an end.

Week Six

"Eeek" "Eeek" "Eeek."

Mom put down her newspaper. "Oh, for the love of Pete. If that incessant sound doesn't stop I swear I'm going to let those gerbils loose in a field somewhere."

"They need the big running ball that's made of clearness," I told her for the fiftieth time.

"They're runners. They need to train.
You know, like Daddy when he decided
he was going to run that marathon and
he got up early to run for nine whole
days in a row before he said that his old

football injury was acting up and maybe running just wasn't his thing?
Well they're like that only without football. And they can run for more than nine days."

"Just for the record, I found a good training program and I did run that race," Daddy said. "Sure, my pace wasn't great but when I say I'm going to do something, I do it."

"Really? Does that include oiling that gerbil wheel?" Mom asked.

She was using her "I'm about to make an issue out of this" voice. When Mom is annoyed she makes me clean my room and then she goes through my toys and tries to make me get rid of the broken ones.

This was not the way I wanted to start my summer vacation, that's for sure.

• • •

"You know what the best thing is about the running ball made of clearness?" I asked no one in particular, "You can take the gerbils outside so they're not cooped up in the house all day making people crazy".

Really the best thing about the running ball made of clearness was that it had air holes so the gerbils wouldn't die while they were in it, but I thought it was best not to rehash old issues right then.

Plus, Mom is all about being outside in the fresh air and not "cooped up" so I thought that was really the best angle to take.

"Fine," Mom said, "We'll get them a running ball when we go out to the store today. But we're not getting them a million things. Just a running ball so I can regain my sanity."

"Well, really, we'll need two," I said. "Otherwise I'll have to mush them both in one ball and I don't know if that meets federal safety guidelines. You know, those rules we can't break, like why I can't sit on Molly's lap in her car seat so we can both go places in her dad's little red car that's too small for kids.

"The one her mom said he got so he could have 'time without the kids'.

"The one they always fight about.

"Anyway, we need two running balls made of clearness. For the safety. And the fighting."

* * *

Mom made a deep sigh again but I knew I had her.

She's a stickler for safety, that woman.

Week Seven

Man, those gerbils could run.

I would put Grizabella in a ball at the end of the driveway and just let her go and she'd run like crazy. Some of that might have been because the driveway was sloped just a little bit so the ball would kind of get rolling on its own, but I really think she liked to run.

She never complained about old injuries and she never said she needed new running shoes when she lost a race to Floyd. She was a good competitor and she just loved being out there running with the wind in her fur in her big ball of clearness.

Being the new parent of gerbils I had to pay attention to their likes and dislikes. They liked driveway marathon running in the ball of clearness. They did not like the Waterfall Game.

The Waterfall Game involved putting Grizabella and Floyd inside their balls of clearness and then putting them at the top of the stairs.

Then I'd let them run to the bottom of the stairs. Only they didn't really run down the waterfall stairs as much as they kind of bounced.

Grizabella always looked a bit dizzy
when she got to the bottom and she sort
of walked sideways for a while.

Mom called it a bad choice and she reminded me that gerbils are living creatures, which I totally knew. I told her that people go down waterfalls in barrels. I saw it on Discovery Channel with Daddy.

I guess it's just not a good choice for gerbils, but I'm totally doing it myself when I'm old enough. And when they make a big ball of clearness that's people sized so I can see where I'm going.

Floyd and Grizabella also weren't huge fans of dancing, which was a shock to me because I can't imagine anyone not wanting to dance around in a tutu all day long.

I put my tutu on so they would understand that I was the dance teacher.

Then I made them each a tutu of their own out of toilet paper.

What I did was, I colored some toilet paper pink with my markers so they'd know it's a tutu and not just a wad of toilet paper.

Then I wrapped each one with a toilet paper tutu and I held them up by their little front legs and I got them dancing.

But, then the toilet paper started to unravel into these long streamers, which made me think of those dancers who hang from long silk scarves and swing from them and flip around and stuff.

Mom and Dad took me to a show last year where people did that. I liked the show so much that I tried to do it too by swinging from a scarf off of the top of the swing set.

Mom said she's never taking me to a show like that again.

But when I tried to tie the toilet paper to the chair and swing Floyd, the paper broke and she looked pretty angry when she landed on the floor.

So, then I tried to use the pink fabric belt from my Easter dress but that was too narrow and I thought it was going to mush Floyd's stomach when I tied it, so then I tried Mom's scarf.

That worked pretty well until Mom came in the room. The gerbils ended up back in their cages and I got a time out.

That woman has no appreciation for the arts I tell you.

• • •

I thought about putting them on little leashes, or putting them both in the running ball, but in the end I decided to let them out so they could really let their creative juices flow.

They did.

They flew under the couch.

And behind the plant in the corner.

And behind the tv that I can't get behind because I'm not two inches wide or a gerbil.

. . .

Finally, Dad got them out and put them back into the cage. He said something about responsibility but really, I was being totally responsible.

I was the best kind of dance teacher there is.

The kind that gives students their freedom.

When I'm in dance class I don't get to hide behind a plant. I tried hiding behind the curtains during the recital last year but Miss Lucy, my teacher, made me come out and take a bow. That's not freedom at all.

That's being forced to take a bow.

· · ·

But my parents didn't quite see it my
way and they put some kind of fastener
on the cage so I couldn't get it open.
That was okay though, because soon
enough, there was so much activity going
on in that cage that I didn't even think
about dance classes anymore.

Week Eight

Grizabella is a boy.

This was not part of the plan.

When we took the gerbils home, Mrs. Moore told us they were both girls.

There was no reason to question her on this. After all, who would name a boy Snuffy or Furball? Those are both clearly girl names.

Well, I guess technically you could call a boy those names, but it would probably hurt his feelings.

Boy gerbils should have names like Scar and Buddy, just so it's clear.

One day Floyd looked a little fat.

The next day, she looked a little fatter.

I didn't really think much of it because
I've read "The Very Hungry Caterpillar"
and that thing gets ginormous before it
eats a leaf and things go back to normal.

But, Mom said it's not like that with gerbils and she got a funny look on her face.

"I think she's going to have some babies," Mom told me.

She said it with that look on her face that she gets when she and Daddy talk about the roof needing work or that weird sound the pipe makes when we flush the downstairs toilet.

"Babies!?" I could hardly contain myself. I had visions of little tiny balls of fur rolling around making happy baby gerbil sounds. "Will they need bottles?" I asked. "What about diapers? We should probably have some sort of a baby shower like Aunt Lydia did so that they can get the things they need." It was weird that they called it a shower when they really meant a party and nobody was showering at all, but there were presents involved, and that was what mattered.

"Only we'll say 'no clothes' because gerbils really don't need clothes, except for maybe a tutu, and plus Aunt Lydia said that everyone sends clothes when what you really need are diapers and a baby swing. A swing! We need a swing!"

"Hold it right there," Mom said. "We're not getting diapers, swings or anything else for those baby gerbils. As soon as they're ready to be weaned, they're going to a pet shop. Or I'm leaving them in a box on your teacher's doorstep."

That didn't seem like the right kind of attitude to have toward being a gerbil grandparent at all.

In fact, it made me think that Mom really had killed Slinky and Slimy, my favorite worms ever.

That woman has a dark side.

• • •

Mom told me that gerbils have lots and lots of babies and that once they start having them, they don't stop. You can end up with hundreds of baby gerbils if you're not careful.

Mom said this like it was a bad thing.

I went into my closet and got out my very smallest toy strollers from my Littlest Pet Shop and started to dust them off.

"If we're going to have hundreds of babies, we really should start getting ready," I told Mom. "You might even have to take some time off from work to help out around here. It's a big job and I can't do it all myself."

Mom deep sighed and left the room.

Week Nine

Grizabella is the worst father ever.

It didn't start off that way. Floyd got bigger and bigger and bigger until I knew it was time to prepare for the big day.

Any time I ask, which is a lot, Daddy and Mom tell me the story of when I was born.

Mom did this thing called "hypnobirthing" which is supposed to make you all relaxed and happy when your baby is born.

My mom isn't ever really relaxed so it's hard for me to think that she had a good plan there, but she says before she had me she was relaxed all the time, so who knows. People change.

Anyway, she did this thing where they played soft music and she took a long bath and they just waited for me to decide to show up.

And then after a lot of hours and a lot of deep breaths, I did show up and they both kissed me and then called down to the hospital cafeteria for a meatball sub for Mom and an extra large coffee for Dad.

And that was it.

Sometimes I think they might have left out some details, but this is the story they always tell and it's never changed, so it must be true.

* * *

So, when it was time I knew what to do.

First I found my most relaxing music.

Mom says that every song I like makes her want to poke herself in the eye, so I decided to go with the classics. "Twinkle Twinkle," "Baby Beluga" and a few others that could make a gerbil really relax.

I didn't force Floyd into a bath, but I did give her an extra big bowl of water just in case it seemed like something she'd want.

Then, I gave her some privacy.

Actually, I was invited to go to a swim party with my best friend, Molly, so giving Floyd her space just kind of worked out.

• • •

And, when I came home, Floyd was looking all relaxed and even kind of proud with five little blobs under her.

They didn't look like gerbils at all.

They were pink and wrinkled and they had no fur and their little eyes were closed and they kind of looked like weird little tiny pig creatures.

I mean, I loved them from the start, don't get me wrong, but they were some strange little things.

Mom went out and got Grizabella his own cage.

She said she'd had it with this nonsense and she wasn't about to start a gerbil breeding farm and the two of them would be separate from now on.

To be honest, I think Grizabella was happy to have some space to himself. But, I was sure that Grizabella would want to meet his babies and it seemed wrong to keep him from them. So, I took Grizabella out of his cage and I dropped him gently into Floyd's cage.

"Grizabella, meet your babies," I said.

He must have heard me wrong.

What he did next was (and this is almost too awful for words so if you're easily grossed out, stop here) he went over to one of his babies.

And before anyone could stop him, Grizabella ate it.

In one glump.

There one second, gone the next.

"Grizabella!" I yelled as I grabbed him and pulled him away,

"I said 'meet your babies,' not 'eat your babies!'"

I put him back in his cage for a time out and then I counted the survivors.

There were still four left.

Floyd didn't seem to care that one of her babies was gone. She didn't even seem to notice. I tried not to take this as a sign that she was a terrible parent.

I figured it had been a long day and she was really tired. But, Grizabella? I did not expect that kind of behavior from him.

When I told Daddy about it he said that it's actually very common and that is why you need to keep the father gerbils in separate cages when their babies are little.

He said it a bit too calmly, like this wasn't the weirdest, grossest thing in the whole world. Then he said something about the circle of life, gave me a hug, and went outside to mow the lawn.

As for me, I listened to the whole soundtrack to *The Lion King* in memory of the little baby gerbil and I played "Circle of Life" really loud and I might have cried a little.

And then I started to work on my next plan: Operation Keep All the Babies Forever.

Week Ten

Operation Keep All The Babies Forever would have worked much better if I hadn't accidentally on purpose let all the babies out the first Thursday in August.

We were getting ready to go on our annual summer camping trip and I was trying to prove to Mom and Daddy that the gerbils could come with us.
I had been working hard to train the baby gerbils to stay together and follow directions.

I figured Floyd and Grizabella just got off on the wrong track because they didn't have a strong parent in their lives until now.

Classroom gerbils get poked a lot and it has to affect them in some pretty bad ways. But these babies would be a different story.

They were getting bigger and fluffier and cuter and they were pretty good listeners as long as you were saying things like, "dig in the sawdust" or "climb on your Mommy".

• • •

The day before our camping trip I decided to show off their listening skills so Mom and Dad would have no choice but to let us bring them camping.

I had visions of putting them all on little leashes and taking them for walks down the trails to the lake, or building little rafts for them and putting their little food pellets on a stick for them to roast over the campfire while I was toasting smores.

It didn't work out that way.

I decided that the kitchen was the best place to show off their skills because it's pretty open and their little nails sound neat on the linoleum.

I scooped all four babies up with a box top and then I placed them gently on the floor. As soon as they hit the ground though, they vroomed away.

I didn't think those little guys could move so fast, but man they were quick.

I thought about telling Mom and Dad right away but Dad was upset that he couldn't find the travel grill and he kept mumbling something about how this was supposed to be the whole point of having a travel grill.

And Mom kept saying that they have grills there at the campsite and let's just go and Dad was still looking and Mom was deep sighing and it just didn't seem like a good time to bring it up.

So instead, I tried to find the gerbils myself.

Our house is big.

Really, really, big.

And baby gerbils are small.

Really, really small.

. . .

In the end, I had to tell Mom and Dad
because they were loading up the car
and I knew we couldn't just take off
with the babies loose in the house.

Mom and Dad loved those little guys as
much as I did, in their own way, and I
knew they'd be heartbroken if anything
happened to them.

"Are you honestly telling me we have
four baby gerbils loose in our kitchen?"
Mom asked as if she didn't really
understand what I had just told her.

I nodded and watched as she thought
through the problem.

Mom and Dad exchanged a look and for a second I thought they were going to just get in the car and make us all go, leaving the gerbils alone in the house for a week.

But, then Mom deep sighed and I knew we were all in this together.

It was Dad who came up with the idea of "Follow the Crunch".

We all sat super quietly on the kitchen floor and listened for the sound of baby gerbils chewing through the sides of boxes.

Luckily for us, baby gerbils are loud
chewers. And they like strong cheese.
So, we followed the sound of chewing
from the cabinets and then we broke out
the cheese and when the little guys got
curious and came out, we grabbed them
and put them back in the cage.

It only took us a few hours, which I
thought was pretty good, but Mom kept

deep sighing and saying at this rate we'd never get our tent up before dark.

She kept talking about getting a cat and setting it loose in the kitchen and just putting an end to this madness.

If I thought for a second that she'd let me keep the cat I might have tried to figure out a way to make that work, but four dead gerbils and a borrowed cat was not a great deal at all.

So, in the end I just kept going with the "follow the chewing sounds" strategy until by some miracle we got them all back in the cage.

"When we get back those gerbils are going," Mom said as we drove down the road.

It was the first thing she said since we got in the car.

I didn't say anything but I knew she was probably right. Those babies needed homes where they could find the love and support they needed to grow up right.

I had a week of summer camp coming up and I couldn't really trust Mom to give the babies the kind of attention that would help them to grow into productive members of gerbil society. After all, that hadn't worked out so well for Slinky and Slimy.

It was time for a new plan.

Sell The Baby Gerbils.

Week Eleven

"**Nobody** is going to buy baby gerbils," Mom said.

Mom also said that nobody would buy lemonade last February when I got bored during vacation and decided to open a stand at the end of the driveway.

But six neighbors who were out shoveling their driveways bought lemonade from me in less than an hour.

And that's when it hit me.

It only took me about an hour to find a big cardboard box to make the stand. I wished Mom had let me keep the stand from last winter but she's not really into clutter and after I kept trying to make her pay me a quarter every time she came through the living room the thing disappeared.

But, before long I had made a new stand, better than ever, with a new sign up on top.

Lemonade and Gerbils
10 Cents Each

I thought about making the gerbils a dollar each but they were still very small and I didn't want to push my luck.

I set up the stand at the end of the driveway and then I waited. I was sure those gerbils would be scooped up in minutes, but after an hour I had only sold two glasses of lemonade and the gerbils were starting to chew on their cardboard box under the stand.

• • •

Finally, after what seemed like forever, I got my big break. It was a little girl on a scooter and her dad.

Dads are way better than moms when it comes to buying things like gerbils. I'm not sure why that is, but it's true.

"Lemonade! Gerbils! Come And Get 'Em!" I called out to the girl and her dad.

They both stopped.

"Did you say 'gerbils'?" He asked.

I nodded. "They're very cute and very small and they don't come when you call them at all but that's okay because you can get them a big ball of clearness to run in and then you can always find them and they won't go under the couch."

"You're selling lemonade and gerbils?" he asked again.

I wasn't sure what the confusion was, unless he thought I meant that they should eat the gerbils to go with the lemonade, but even Grizabella seemed to have stopped thinking about eating the gerbils.

"Yup, lemonade and gerbils. My mom made the lemonade because I put in too much mix when I do it, and Floyd and Grizabella made the gerbils."

"They were supposed to both be girl gerbils but then they weren't and now we have babies and Mom said 'enough is enough' and even though they're cute she doesn't want me to even keep just one, so I'm selling them here with the lemonade."

I pulled out the box from under the stand.

"See?" I held up one little, fuzzy baby gerbil and that was all it took. I knew the look on the girl's face.

I am an expert at that look. I practically invented that look.

I knew what was coming next.

The girl turned to her father.

"Daddy, pleeeease? Pleeease can I have the gerbils? Pleeeese? I'll never ask for anything else ever and I won't leave my scooter in the driveway and I'll take good care of them and you won't even know they're there and it will be the best thing ever. Pleeeease!?"

The dad didn't say "no" right away and that's when I knew.

The gerbils were going to a new home.

The little babies that I had cared for and loved would be moving on to new adventures. I wanted to keep just one, to slip a little ball of fur into my pocket, but I knew that the gerbil babies needed to stay together.

Floyd and Grizabella would be headed back to school at the end of the summer and the babies would only have each other. It wouldn't be fair to split up the family.

"We'll take two of them, as long as they're both the same gender," the dad said.

So much for not splitting up the family.

I thought about everything that the babies had been through together; the tragic loss of their little brother or sister, the adventures in the kitchen, the tutus, and I knew I'd have to play this right.

"Actually, all four of them are girls," I said. I had no idea if they were boys or girls, but I figured I couldn't really be telling a lie if I didn't know what was true.

It was more like telling them what they wanted to hear so they would adopt all the gerbils together and give them a good home.

"They've never been apart from each other," I continued.

"Every night they snuggle into a tight ball and every day they play games together. Their favorite game is 'roll on top of each other' but I'm sure you could teach them more."

The little girl looked at her father.

I went on, "There's really no difference between two gerbils and four. They don't eat much and they're super cute."
I paused for effect. "I'd hate to see the family broken up."

The father deep sighed and gave me a five-dollar bill. I thought that was more than fair.

After giving each gerbil a little pat I handed over the box and the little baby gerbils went scooting off to their new home.

Week Twelve

The house was quiet without the babies.

I could tell that Floyd was feeling the void but Grizabella didn't seem to care. He was still in his own cage where Mom said he'd stay until he and Floyd went back to school.

He spent most of his time running on his big wheel that went "Eeek" "Eeek" and sleeping.

Floyd still went out for runs in the big ball of clearness but summer was winding down and I knew she was itching to get back to school.

I wasn't enough to keep them entertained after all the excitement of the summer and I knew it.

They were both ready to get back to the classroom, to meet a new set of kids, even if it meant getting poked by some other Mark Pitts kind of boy or being called "Fluffy" by some little first grade girl.

I was older now and I was ready for the adventures of second grade.

My new teacher didn't have any pets, which made me kind of sad, but it also helped me a bit when it came to my one final mission of the summer.

* * *

I found Mom outside washing her car.

"So, Mom, the house is going to be pretty quiet when Floyd and Grizabella leave, isn't it?"

"Mercifully so," she said.

"You have to admit, they are pretty cute," I said. "Sure, they don't really do much and it's not like I could really play with them or anything, but they were good company for an only child like me," I said.

I picked up a sponge and started to help her suds up her car.

"I know what you're doing," Mom said.

"You mean helping you wash the car?"

"I mean pulling the, 'I need a baby brother or sister' card again."

"Not a baby brother," I said.
"We've talked about this. It has to be a girl."

"We've talked about this and we're having neither. It's just you kiddo," Mom said.

"I guess hoping for a little sister was too much to ask," I said sadly.

I waited for a long time before I continued.

I had to play this one right.

The gerbils were a good first step, a trial run, and overall I thought it had gone pretty well.

Aside from the one that had been eaten and the babies getting loose and some of the costume issues when they were dancers.

I was a good gerbil parent and it was just a matter of time before Mom saw that. I had kept them alive all summer long and I had even sold all of the babies to a stranger on the street. All for one reason.

One larger mission that would be the mission to end all missions.

I took a deep breath and then I turned toward Mom. As casually as I could, I let the words flow from my tongue.

"Molly's cat just had kittens."

Mom deep sighed but deep inside I knew.

This was going to be the start of another great adventure.

About the Authors

Elaine Miskinis writes and teaches English in Exeter, New Hampshire, and as a mother of two young girls is surrounded by discussions ranging from burial procedures for worms to tutu materials for gerbils. This is her world.

In addition to teaching and writing novels, Elaine has written for magazine publications ranging from "Educational Leadership" to "American Careers," has been invited to speak about education and literature at The National Council of Teachers of English national conference several times, and her TEDx Talk, "Three Lies We Tell Children" was selected as a TED Talk of the Month by TED.com.

Lorrie Moore began her professional career as an animation cleanup artist for Creative Capers Entertainment, where she worked on animation for numerous projects for Disney Interactive. She later went on to co-create the Zodiac Girlz, a line of tween-oriented dolls with accompanying merchandise. She has an action figure of herself.

In addition to her work as a character designer and illustrator, she has developed many video game character concept designs for WhiteMoon Dreams, a video game production company located in Pasadena, California.

Leena and the Gerbils is proudly presented in Dyslexie Font, a typeface designed to make reading easier and more enjoyable for readers with dyslexia. Learn more at dyslexiefont.com

Don't miss the next Leena book!

Find more and please stay in touch at
elainemiskinis.com

Thank you so much for reading!

Made in the USA
Columbia, SC
27 January 2018